My Weird School #11

Mrs. Kormel Is Not Normal!

Dan Gutman

Pictures by
Jim Paillot

HarperCollins*Publishers*

Library of Congress Cataloging-in-Publication Data is available.

ISBN-10: 0-06-082229-5 (pbk.) — ISBN-13: 978-0-06-082229-3 (pbk.)

ISBN-10: 0-06-082230-9 (lib. bdg.) — ISBN-13: 978-0-06-082230-9 (lib. bdg.)

1 2 3 4 5 6 7 8 9 10

❖

First Edition

To Emma

Contents

Never Kiss Your Mom in Public

My name is A.J. and I hate school.

Do you know which is the worst day of the week? If you ask me, it's Monday. Because Monday is the start of five days of school in a row. That's horrible!

Tuesday and Wednesday aren't so great either.

Thursday is a pretty good day, because then we only have one day of school left before the weekend.

Friday is *really* good, because that's when the school week is over.

But the best day of the week is Saturday. I play peewee football on Saturday, and we don't have school again for two whole days.

Too bad it was Monday morning. I was waiting in front of my house for the school bus with my mom.

"You be a good boy, A.J.," my mom told me.

"I will."

"Don't get into any trouble, A.J.," my mom told me.

"I won't."

"Remember to raise your hand when you want to talk, A.J.," my mom told me.

"I will."

"Don't shoot straw wrappers at the girls, A.J.," my mom told me.

"I won't."

My mom told me about a million hundred other things I wasn't allowed to do until I saw the yellow school bus coming around the corner.

"Mom, I promise not to have any fun at all," I said. "Bye!"

The bus pulled up. Mrs. Kormel, the

bus driver, pushed a button and made the little STOP sign pop out the side of the bus so the cars on the street will stop. We call it the magic STOP sign. That thing is cool.

"Give Mommy a kiss, A.J."

No way I was going to kiss my mother in front of all the kids staring out the bus window. That's the first rule of being a kid. Don't *ever* kiss your mother when other kids are watching!

"Uh, I don't want to be late for school, Mom."

"Give Mommy a kiss, A.J."

"That's not gonna happen, Mom."

"Give Mommy a kiss, A.J."

"Over my dead body, Mom."

"Give Mommy a kiss, A.J."

"I will if you give me a hundred dollars, Mom," I said.

My mother tried to wrap her arms around me, but I know how to get away from tacklers. When Mom went to grab me, I threw her a head fake, spun away, and gave her a few of my best fancy foot-work moves that I learned playing peewee football. She didn't have a chance! I sidestepped her and ran on the bus before she could hug or kiss me.

Ha-ha-ha! My mom can't play football for beans. Nah-nah-nah boo-boo on her!

Mrs. Kormel's Secret Language

I dashed on the bus and there was Mrs. Kormel, the school bus driver. She was wearing a crash helmet on her head and a silver whistle around her neck.

"Bingle boo, A.J.!" she said.

"Bingle boo, Mrs. Kormel."

"Bingle boo" is Mrs. Kormel's way of

saying "hello." One time I asked her why she doesn't just say "hello" like normal people.

"I'm inventing my own secret language," she told me. "*Everybody* says 'hello.' But I think 'hello' is boring. I'm trying to get people to switch from saying 'hello'

to saying 'bingle boo.' Secret languages are fun!"

Mrs. Kormel is not normal.

"Limpus kidoodle," said Mrs. Kormel. That means "sit down" in Mrs. Kormel's secret language.

I looked around the bus. There was a snot-covered kindergartner in the front row behind Mrs. Kormel, and a few angry fifth graders in the back row.

Fifth graders are really mean because they get a lot of homework. The more homework you get, the meaner you are. That's why fifth graders are meaner than fourth graders, and fourth graders are meaner than third graders, and third graders are meaner than second graders.

You don't want to go *near* seventh or eighth graders. They get *lots* of homework, and they just hate the world. I hope I never get to high school.

I sat down in the middle by myself. Mrs. Kormel stopped the bus at the next corner, and a few other kids got on. At the stop after that, my friends Ryan and Michael got on.

"Bingle boo!" Mrs. Kormel said to Ryan and Michael. "Limpus kidoodle."

Ryan and Michael sat down next to me.

"What did you bring in for Show and Share?" Ryan asked. "I brought in an old light switch."

"I brought in a ball of string," said Michael.

Show and Share is when we bring something from home that starts with a certain letter of the alphabet and talk about it in class. Today's letter was *s*.

I took my Show and Share thing out of my backpack. It was an action figure called Striker Smith. He's a superhero from the future who travels through time and fights bad guys with a sharp sword that's attached to his hand. He can turn into a jet plane, too, and fly when you push a button. I saw a commercial for Striker Smith on TV and bugged my parents until they finally got it for me.

"Striker Smith belongs to a secret organization of crime fighters," I told Ryan and Michael, in case they didn't see the commercial.

"You should get extra credit," Ryan said, "because Striker Smith has *two* S's."

"He's cool," said Michael. "Sometimes I take my old action figures down to the basement and my dad lets me saw them in half or torture them with his power drill."

"I take mine out in the sun and melt their faces with a magnifying glass," said Ryan.

Michael and Ryan are weird.

At the next stop, this really annoying girl in my class named Andrea who thinks she knows everything got on the bus with curly brown hair. Well, the bus didn't have curly brown hair. Andrea did.

"Bingle boo, Andrea!" said Mrs. Kormel.

"Bingle boo," Andrea said. "I'll go limpus kidoodle now."

What a brownnoser! Andrea plopped her dumb self down in the seat right in front of me, like always.

"Good morning, Arlo," she said.

I hate her.

Andrea's mother found out that A.J. stands for Arlo Jervis, so Andrea went and told everybody. It was the worst day of my life. I thought I was gonna die. I wanted to switch schools or move to Antarctica and go live with the penguins, but my mom wouldn't let me.

Penguins are cool.

"Are you boys ready for the big spelling test this afternoon?" Andrea asked.

Oh no. I forgot all about the big dumb spelling test! How can I be expected to remember stuff over the weekend? Weekends are for having fun, not for studying for tests. I hate spelling.

"Do you know how to spell 'spelling,' A.J.?" asked Andrea.

"Sure," I said. "I-H-A-T-E-Y-O-U."

Michael and Ryan laughed.

"I made my own spelling flash cards," Andrea told us, "and I'm going to use them for Show and Share, too. Because spelling begins with an *s*."

I was going to tell Andrea that "stupid" also begins with an *s* and that's what she

is, but I decided I would save that and use it the next time she *really* got me mad.

Andrea turned around so she wasn't facing us anymore. I picked up Striker Smith and pretended that he was going to attack the back of her head with his sword. It was hilarious. Michael and Ryan laughed. But Andrea turned around suddenly, before I could take Striker Smith away from her head.

"That's a nice doll, Arlo," she said.

"It's not a doll!" I told her. "It's an action figure!"

"My mother told me that action figures are dolls for boys," said Andrea.

"They are not!" I said.

"Are too!" said Andrea.

We went back and forth like that for a while.

"Striker Smith is a one-man wrecking machine," I told Andrea. "He belongs to a secret organization of crime fighters. If Striker got into a fight with one of your dumb dolls, he would rip its head off."

"Dolls don't fight," Andrea said.

"Striker Smith does," I said.

"I thought you said he wasn't a doll, Arlo."

Why can't a bus filled with spelling flash cards fall on Andrea's head?

3

My Head Almost Exploded

"Bingle boo! Limpus kidoodle," said Mrs. Kormel.

Andrea's equally annoying crybaby friend Emily got on the bus in front of her house. She sat down next to Andrea, and they studied Andrea's dumb flash cards together.

"Is everybody here?" asked Mrs. Kormel after she picked up a few more kids.

"Yes," we all said.

"If you're not here, raise your hand."

I knew that was a trick question, because if somebody wasn't there we wouldn't be able to see if their hand was up. But just to be on the safe side, I got up in my seat to see if anybody who wasn't there had their hand up.

"Limpus kidoodle, A.J.," said Mrs. Kormel.

In case you don't remember, that means "sit down." Mrs. Kormel doesn't like it when we get out of our seats.

"No standing on the seats," said Mrs. Kormel.

"Can I kneel on my seat?" I asked.

"You can only kneel on your seat if your name is Neil. Anyone named Neil may kneel."

"Can I stand if my name is Stan?" asked Ryan.

"Okay," said Mrs. Kormel. "If your name

is Stan, you can stand."

"I can't stand sitting down," Michael said.

"Nobody can stand sitting down," Ryan said. "If you're sitting down, you're not standing."

"Can you crouch if your name is Crouch?" I asked.

"There's nobody named Crouch!" Andrea told me. She thinks she knows everything.

"Oh yeah?" I said. "What about that guy on Sesame Street named Oscar the Crouch?"

"That's Oscar the *Grouch*, dumbhead!" Andrea said.

I knew that.

"Now that we're all here, how about singing a song to make the ride go quicker?" suggested Mrs. Kormel.

"Let's sing 'The Wheels on the Bus'!" said Andrea. "I love that song."

"I hate that song," I said. "Can we sing 'Ninety-nine Bottles of Beer on the Wall'?"

Mrs. Kormel said we couldn't sing about beer because kids aren't allowed to drink beer. I wouldn't want to drink beer even if I was allowed to. My dad gave me a sip of his beer once. I thought I was gonna throw up. Mrs. Kormel said we could sing "Ninety-nine Bottles of Pop on the Wall" if we wanted to.

The girls started singing "The Wheels

on the Bus." The boys
"Ninety-nine Bottles of Pop
Me and Michael and Ryan t
louder than all the girls. An
Emily tried to sing louder than
boys. It was really *loud* in there.

Soon everybody on the bus was scream-
ing, and kids were bouncing around like
Mexican jumping beans. I covered my ears
so my head wouldn't explode.

Something about being on a school
bus makes you want to go crazy. Maybe
it's all that yellow.

I'll bet Mrs. Kormel was sorry she told
us to sing. Suddenly she blew her whistle
really loud.

"Zingy zip!" she yelled.

That's her way of saying "quiet down" in her secret language. Everybody stopped singing.

"Shhhhh, my cell phone is ringing," said Mrs. Kormel. "It's Mr. Klutz."

Mr. Klutz is our principal. He is like the king of the school. He's bald, too. One time he kissed a pig. This other time he got stuck on the top of the flagpole. Another time he was climbing the school, and the custodian had to rescue him by sticking one of those toilet plungers on his head. We saw it live and in person. Mr. Klutz is nuts!

"What does Mr. Klutz want?" somebody yelled.

Mrs. Kormel finished talking to Mr. Klutz and turned around to whisper something to the boy in the row behind her. He turned around and whispered something to the girl in the row behind him. She turned and whispered something to the girl in the row across from her, who then turned and whispered something to Michael.

"We have to go pick up a nude kid," Michael whispered.

"A nude kid?" I said. "That's disgusting!"

"That nude kid better not sit next to me," said Ryan.

"Tell the nude kid to put some clothes on!" said Michael.

Are We There Yet?

We hadn't even met him yet, but suddenly everybody on the bus was buzzing about the nude kid.

"Some people don't believe in wearing clothes," said Andrea, who thinks she knows everything. "They're called nudists."

"I call 'em freaks," said Ryan.

"My parents say we should respect and celebrate people's differences," Emily said.

"Your parents are weird," I told her.

"What's the big deal?" Andrea asked. "After all, we were born without clothing."

"You were born without a brain," I couldn't resist adding. Anytime anyone says anything about being born, always say they were born without a brain. That's the first rule of being a kid.

"I'm nude under my clothes," Ryan told us.

"Thanks for sharing that with us," I told him. "Now I'm totally grossed out."

Andrea said that nudists save a lot of

money because they don't have to buy clothes. But Michael said that nudists have to spend a lot of money because they always have to buy sunscreen. But Emily said that nudists save a lot of money because they don't have to do laundry. But Ryan said that nudists have to spend a lot of money to heat their houses because they're so cold.

"The nude kid probably doesn't even have a closet at home," I said, "because he doesn't have any clothes to put in it."

"Do you think nude kids are allowed to wear hats?" asked Michael.

"Zingy zip!" yelled Mrs. Kormel.

Mrs. Kormel had pulled out a big map and she had it opened up on top of the steering wheel. She told us we had to be quiet while she figured out the directions. I bet it's hard to drive and look at a map at the same time.

To make things even worse, it started raining. Mrs. Kormel put the windshield wipers on. All the girls started to sing,

"'The wipers on the bus go *swish swish swish, swish swish swish, swish swish swish*!'"

"Zingy zip!" Mrs. Kormel yelled again. "I can't concentrate."

We drove for a long time in the rain. It was hard to go so long without talking.

"Are we there yet?" somebody asked.

"No," said Mrs. Kormel.

"Are we lost?" Emily asked.

"Of course not," said Mrs. Kormel. "I just don't know where we are."

"Oh no, we're going to miss Show and Share!" Andrea said to Emily, like she was all worried. "And I spent all weekend making my spelling flash cards."

Ha-ha-ha! I spent all weekend playing football. Nah-nah-nah boo-boo on her! We were going to be late for school. It was great! I hoped Mrs. Kormel wouldn't find the right way to the nude kid's house for a while. Because right after Show and Share, we have math.

And I hate math.

The Middle of Nowhere

Mrs. Kormel drove for a million hundred hours, and we *still* hadn't reached the nude kid's house. Where *was* it? Now Show and Share was over for sure. We probably missed math, too. If we didn't get to school soon, we would miss our DEAR time. That stands for Drop Everything and Read.

I hate reading.

Finally we drove by some big trucks and there was a sign that said DETOUR.

"Hey, we're going to take a tour," said Ryan. "Tours are cool!"

"Detours aren't tours, dumbhead!" said Andrea. "Workers are fixing the road, so Mrs. Kormel has to get off this road and go another way to the nude kid's house."

"Bix blattinger!" said Mrs. Kormel as she slammed her fist against the steering wheel.

I don't know what "bix blattinger" means, but that's what Mrs. Kormel

always says when she gets really angry or frustrated.

"What does 'bix blattinger' mean, Mrs. Kormel?" I asked.

"Never you mind!" said Mrs. Kormel.

"I think Mrs. Kormel must have said a bad word," said Ryan.

"But she said it in her secret language," Michael said, "so we won't know what it means."

You shouldn't say bad words. We all tried to figure out which bad word Mrs. Kormel said. I had heard most

of the bad words, but Michael and Ryan knew a few that I didn't know and they taught them to me. So even though we were really late for school, it was still a learning experience.

After we got off the regular road, the road we were on wasn't even a real road. It was more like a jungle or a swamp or something. There were these big plants slapping against the bus windows. The ride was bumpy, and it was still raining. Mrs. Kormel could barely see in front of her.

"This is like the rainforest," Andrea said.

"I hope we don't get eaten by alligators," said Michael.

"Look!" somebody yelled. A family of ducks was crossing the road in front of us.

"They're cute!" shouted all the girls.

"Let's run them over!" shouted all the boys.

I didn't *really* want Mrs. Kormel to run

over the ducks, but it was hilarious anyway.

Mrs. Kormel kept on driving, but I didn't see the nude kid's house anywhere. In fact, I didn't see *any* houses. Or human beings.

"Where *are* we?" somebody asked.

"The middle of nowhere," said Mrs. Kormel.

I said it was too bad we weren't at the *edge* of nowhere. Because if we were at the edge of nowhere, we'd be right next to the edge of somewhere. And the edge of somewhere is near the middle of somewhere, which is where we wanted to be.

Ryan said we were probably close to the nude kid's house. Because if you were nude, you'd probably live in the middle of nowhere. That way, nobody would see you. And that's where we were. It made sense to me.

Andrea looked at her watch and got all upset.

"We missed DEAR time!" she complained. "We're very late for school now."

Ha-ha-ha! This was the greatest day of my life!

"Don't worry, Andrea," said Mrs. Kormel. "I'll get you to school if it's the last thing I do."

Just then I had a genius thought. Right after DEAR time is spelling. I hate spelling. And if we'd missed DEAR time and we weren't even at the nude kid's house yet, there was a good chance that we were going to miss spelling, too. And that meant we would miss the big spelling test, which I didn't study for!

I decided that the nude kid was the coolest kid in the history of the world. Thanks to him, we were going to miss the big spelling test.

"Bix blattinger!" said Mrs. Kormel.

"Ooooh!" we all said. "Mrs. Kormel said that bad word again!"

The Nude Kid's Dad

Finally Mrs. Kormel stopped the bus in front of a house and pushed the button to make the magic STOP sign pop out.

"This must be the nude kid's house," Ryan said.

It looked like a pretty normal house. There was a swing set on the lawn and a car in the driveway. You would never know that nudists lived there.

Nobody came out of the house, so Mrs. Kormel honked the horn. We all craned our necks to get a look at the nude kid, but he didn't come out.

"Where *is* he?" Ryan asked.

Suddenly the front door of the house opened. A guy came out with an umbrella. And it was the most amazing thing in the history of the world. You know why?

Because the guy had clothes on!

The guy with clothes on came over to the bus. He climbed up the steps and said something to Mrs. Kormel.

"Bix blattinger!" muttered Mrs. Kormel

after the guy got off the bus. She was probably mad at Mr. Klutz because he made her drive all the way out to the nude kid's house and the nude kid wasn't even there.

"What did he say?" we all asked. "What did he say?"

"He said his wife drove their son to school today on her way to work," Mrs. Kormel told us. "She didn't want him to be late on his first day of school."

"Maybe she took him to buy some clothes," said Michael.

Mrs. Kormel closed the bus door and made the magic STOP sign go back. Before the nude kid's dad went inside his house, me and Ryan leaned out the window and yelled to him.

"Hey, mister! Do you sleep with clothes on and then take them off after you wake up?"

"Where does your son keep his lunch money if he doesn't have pockets?"

It was hilarious. The nude kid's dad just looked at us with this confused expression on his face. Then he went inside.

Nudists are weird.

Fighting Evil Under the Bus

Finally we were back on the road. Mrs. Kormel was mad at Mr. Klutz for making her drive to the nude kid's house for nothing. I was mad because we would be at school soon. Andrea was mad because spelling was over and she didn't get the chance to take the big spelling test and show everybody how smart she was. Well, nah-nah-nah boo-boo on Andrea! She would go to school on the weekend if it was open.

The rain stopped. I was getting hungry. We had missed snack time. It was probably close to lunchtime. We were bored, too, and sick of sitting on the bus.

Ryan flipped his light switch on and off. Michael played with his ball of string. I played with Striker Smith. That's when I got the most genius idea in the history of the world! We could tie Michael's string

to Striker Smith's leg and fly him out the window!

Michael and Ryan realized what a genius I was. We tied the string to Striker Smith and opened the window.

"You're going to get in trouble, A.J.," said Andrea. "We're not supposed to hold things out the window."

"Can you possibly be any more boring?" I asked Andrea. "We're

not holding anything out the window. The string will hold him."

Ryan tossed Striker Smith out the window.

"Look!" Ryan said. "He's flying!"

It was cool. Striker Smith was doing loops in the air. You should have been there.

"He's fighting evil outside the bus!" said Michael.

"Mrs. Kormel!" Andrea whined. "A.J. threw his doll out the window!"

"It's not a doll!" I told Andrea. "It's an action figure. And it's none of your beeswax."

What is her problem?

It didn't matter what Andrea said,

because Mrs. Kormel didn't hear her anyway. Striker Smith was flying outside the bus, dipping and diving in the wind. He is so cool.

The only problem was that suddenly Striker Smith dove down so far that we couldn't see him anymore.

"Where is he?" asked Ryan.

"He's fighting evil under the bus," I said.

But I don't think Striker Smith was fighting evil under the bus. Because that's when I heard a pop, and then a hissing sound.

Hisssssssss!

Striker Smith's Final Battle

Ryan pulled the string up. There was nothing on the other end! Striker Smith was gone!

Suddenly the ride got all bumpy. Mrs. Kormel pulled off the side of the road. She opened the door and got out to see what was the matter.

"You're in big trouble, A.J.," Andrea said.

"So is your face," I replied.

Mrs. Kormel came back on the bus. She was holding Striker Smith in her hand. Or what was left of him, anyway. His head was gone. So was one of his legs and the arm that used to hold his sword.

I felt bad. My parents probably paid a lot of money to get me this cool action figure, and now it was totally crushed. On the other hand, it is also a well-known fact that crushing stuff and pulling the limbs off action figures is cool.

All in all, I was just happy that Show and Share was over. It wouldn't be very cool to show the class an action figure that was missing an arm, a leg, and his head.

"Who does this belong to?" asked Mrs. Kormel.

Andrea looked at me. I looked at Ryan. Ryan looked at me. Mrs. Kormel looked at me. I didn't know what to say. I didn't know what to do. I had to think fast.

"I said, who does this belong to?"

"Striker Smith belongs to a secret organization of crime fighters," I said.

I thought Mrs. Kormel was going to be really mad. But she just told us all to get off the bus. She said we had a flat tire and she was going to call Mr. Klutz to send somebody out to fix it. In the meantime, we'd have to wait outside.

"Now we're going to miss lunch!" one of the mean fifth graders complained.

"Who cares about lunch?" said some-body else. "We're going to miss recess!"

"It's all Arlo's fault," said Andrea.

"It is not," I said.

"It is too."

"Oh yeah?" I said. "Well, stupid begins with an *s* and that's what *you* are."

Ha-ha-ha! In her face!

We all got off the bus. It was a quiet road, and there were no other cars or houses or people around. Me and Ryan and Michael went to look at the flat tire.

Striker Smith's sword was stuck right in the tire with his arm still attached to it. It was cool. It was like that story "The Sword in the Stone," except with a tire.

Mrs. Kormel tried to call Mr. Klutz on her cell phone, but something was wrong, and she started stamping her feet and yelling.

"Bix blattinger!" she yelled. "My cell phone battery is dead!"

Mrs. Kormel said she would have to fix the flat tire herself. She told us to get our lunches and have a little picnic on the sidewalk while she got out her tools and the spare tire.

Not everybody had brought a lunch bag, because some kids buy the school lunch. They must be nuts. The school lunch is usually rubber hot dogs, chicken nuggets that bounce, and nachos that glow in the dark. I wouldn't eat the school lunch if I was starving and there was no other food left in the world.

Mrs. Kormel asked us to share some of our food with kids who didn't bring a lunch. I gave my tuna sandwich to one of the first graders, but I kept my pudding treat.

I always eat my treat first anyway. You should always eat your treat first because if an asteroid hits the earth in the middle of lunch and destroys the planet, well, at least you got to eat your dessert. That's the first rule of being a kid. It would be a major bummer if the earth was destroyed by an asteroid and you didn't have the chance to eat dessert.

"Hey," Ryan said, "look what I found!"

It was Striker Smith's head! Ryan found it at the side of the road.

We decided right away to hold a funeral for the head. Michael dug a little hole in the dirt, and we dropped the head into it. Some of the other boys on the bus gathered around.

"Farewell, Striker," Ryan said solemnly. "You defeated the mighty tire. You sacrificed your life, so that others might not have to go to school. You paid the ultimate price, made the ultimate sacrifice so that we can live in freedom from reading, writing, and arithmetic. Long live Striker Smith. We will always remember you."

It was really sad. I almost cried when Michael said a little prayer:

Ashes to ashes,
Dust to dusted.
We buried Striker Smith,
Because he was busted.
He was really cool,
But now he's dead.
It's hard to live
When you don't have a head.

We covered up Striker's grave, and Ryan said we should have a moment of silence in honor of our fallen superhero.

It was really quiet. Then, in the middle of our moment of silence, Andrea said, "Boys are dumbheads."

We Are Survivors

Finally Mrs. Kormel fixed the flat tire and said we could get back on the bus. She was all sweaty, and her hair was messed up, and her hands were covered with grease. She looked too tired to be mad at me or Mr. Klutz or anybody else. She just got into her bus driver's seat and hit the

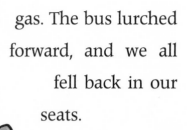

gas. The bus lurched forward, and we all fell back in our seats.

It was really late. Andrea complained that we might have missed social studies. Ha-ha-ha! That was fine with me. I hate social studies. Why is it called social studies anyway?

Mrs. Kormel was driving fast! We were far from school. It looked to me like we were still in the middle of nowhere. The road was really bumpy, and it was wet from the rain. Mrs. Kormel was having trouble keeping the bus in the middle of the road. I was afraid she might drive right off the side of the road.

And what happened next was the most amazing thing in the history of the world.

Do you want to know what happened?

I'm not going to tell you.

Well, okay, I'll tell you.

Mrs. Kormel drove right off the side of the road!

"Bix blattinger!" shouted Mrs. Kormel.

The bus skidded to a stop. Some kids even fell out of their seats! It was hilarious. You should have been there.

"Is everybody okay?" Mrs. Kormel asked.

"Yeah!" me and Michael and Ryan said.

"That was fun. Can we do it again?"

"We're stuck in a ditch," said Mrs. Kormel. "We're not going anywhere."

"What are we going to do *now*?" asked Emily. She looked like she was going to cry. I was amazed that Emily hadn't cried yet. She usually can't go five minutes without crying about *something*.

"I don't know what to do," Mrs. Kormel said sadly. "My cell phone is dead. I guess we'll just have to wait for help to arrive."

"Too bad Striker Smith isn't here," I said. "He would know what to do."

"If you hadn't thrown that dumb doll out the window, none of this would have happened!" yelled Andrea.

"He's not a doll!" I yelled right back at her.

"Zingy zip!" yelled Mrs. Kormel.

Everybody was really depressed. We just sat there on the bus. There was nobody around. No houses. No stores. No nothing. Nobody was going to rescue us. It felt like we had been on the bus a million hundred hours.

It occurred to me that we might not only miss the rest of the school day, we might miss the rest of our *lives*! We could sit there forever. We could die out there!

Suddenly I felt hungry. I wished I hadn't given my sandwich to that first grader. I was starving. I was afraid my stomach might eat itself.

My friend Billy who lives around the

corner from me and was in second grade last year told me he once heard about some guy who was stranded on an airplane, and he ate a seat cushion to survive.

"We might have to eat the seat cushions," I told Michael and Ryan.

Ryan looked at the seat cushion.

There's something you need to know about Ryan. He will eat anything, even stuff that is not food. One time we gave him a dollar to eat dirt.

Ryan got down on the floor and took a little bite from the corner of the cushion.

"Ugh," he said. "It's horrible."

"Put some ketchup on it," suggested Michael. "Ketchup makes anything taste good."

Michael gave Ryan a little ketchup packet from his lunch bag. Ryan put it on the seat cushion and took a tiny bite.

"It's not bad, actually," Ryan said.

Ryan is weird.

It was so boring sitting there waiting for somebody to rescue us. I almost wished we were at school. Almost.

"I saw this reality TV show where some people were stranded on a dessert island," Michael said.

"It's not a *dessert* island, dumbhead,"

Andrea turned around to say. "It's a desert island. One *s*. 'Desserts' is one of our spelling words this week." Then she held up her dumb flash card with the word "desserts" on it.

"Who asked you?" Ryan asked.

"A dessert island would be cool to be stranded on," I said. "There would be ice cream and candy and treats everywhere."

"Hey, look," said Emily, "I just noticed that 'desserts' is 'stressed' spelled backward."

"So what?" asked Ryan. "'Backward' is 'drawkcab' backward."

"Who cares what 'backward' is backward?" asked Andrea.

"'Bus' is 'sub' backward," I mentioned.

"Bix blattinger!" shouted Mrs. Kormel. "Will you please zingy zip?"

I couldn't blame Mrs. Kormel for being mad. It was a rough day for her. We had to whisper after that.

"Hey," whispered Michael, "I just thought of something. Maybe we're on a reality TV show right now and we don't even know it."

"That's impossible," Ryan whispered. "If we didn't know we were on a reality TV show, we wouldn't be talking about us being on a reality TV show."

"I think Michael is right," I said, looking around to see if there were any hidden cameras. "Maybe this was all planned in advance for the reality TV show we're on right now."

"Oh yeah?" said Andrea. "Who planned for you to throw your doll out the window and cause a flat tire?"

"It's not a doll!" I said. "Don't you have any respect for the dead?"

"If this *is* a reality TV show," Ryan said, "we're going to have to vote somebody off the bus."

"Why?" asked Emily.

"Because that's what they *always* do on reality TV shows, dumbhead!" I said. "You vote somebody off and they have to leave."

"But why?" asked Emily.

"Because that's the rule!" Michael told Emily. She doesn't know anything about reality TV shows.

"I vote for Andrea," I said.

"I vote for A.J.," Andrea said.

"Ooooh!" Ryan said. "A.J. and Andrea voted for each other. They must be in *love*!"

"When are you gonna get married?" asked Michael.

If those guys weren't my best friends, I would hate them.

10

Mrs. Kormel Is Driving Us Crazy

We couldn't just sit around on the bus forever. Soon we would die of starvation or kill each other, like they do in the movies all the time.

"We've got to *do* something!" Emily said.

For once she was right. That's when I

got the most genius idea in the history of the world. There must have been at least twenty kids on the bus. If we all got out and pushed, maybe we could push the bus out of the ditch!

I got up and and told Mrs. Kormel about my genius idea. At first she thought I was crazy and told me to go limpus kidoodle. But I guess she thought it over and decided to give it a shot.

"Okay, everybody off the bus!" she yelled.

We all got off the bus and went to the back.

"When I say push, everybody push," Mrs. Kormel yelled out the window.

"One . . . two . . . three . . . PUSH!"

I pushed with all my might. Everybody was grunting and groaning and moaning. The bus didn't move.

"Harder!" yelled Ryan.

And then the most amazing thing in the history of the world happened.

The bus started moving!

"Hooray!" everybody yelled.

Mrs. Kormel steered the bus back onto the road, and we all piled in. She told me my idea was great, and promised to drive carefully the rest of the way to school.

The only one who wasn't happy was Andrea. She was looking at her watch.

"Now we've missed music class," she complained.

That was fine with me. I hate music.

"Y'know," Michael said, "maybe Mrs. Kormel isn't a bus driver at all. Did you ever think of that?"

"Yeah," Ryan said. "Maybe she captured our real bus driver and has her tied up in a cave. Stuff like that happens all the time, you know."

"Stop trying to scare Emily," Andrea said.

"Maybe we're being kidnapped," I added. "Maybe Mrs. Kormel is driving us to her secret underground hideout at the North Pole, where she's going to do unspeakable things to us."

"Like what things?" Emily asked, all worried.

"I can't tell you," I told her. "They're unspeakable!"

"We've got to *do* something!" Emily said. "I don't want to go to the North Pole!"

That girl will fall for everything. Emily probably wanted to run away. But there was no place to run. She was stuck on the bus. So she started crying. What a baby!

Once Emily started crying, it set off a

chain reaction and other kids started crying, too. Some of the first graders said they wanted their mommies. Some kid peed in his pants. Everyone was freaking out.

The fifth graders made a sign and put it in the back window—HELP! OUR BUS DRIVER IS DRIVING US CRAZY!

I didn't cry. I figured that it would be pretty horrible to be kidnapped and driven to the North Pole, but at least we wouldn't have to go to school anymore. And they have penguins at the North Pole too. Or maybe that's the South Pole. Either way, penguins are cool.

"Are we there yet?" somebody asked.

"KNOCK IT OFF!" yelled Mrs. Kormel.

We Finally Meet the Nude Kid

The bus turned a corner, and we saw the big sign—ELLA MENTRY SCHOOL.

"We're there yet!" announced Mrs. Kormel.

"Yippee!" yelled all the girls.

"Boo!" yelled all the boys.

Mrs. Kormel pulled the bus up to the curb, and Mr. Klutz came running over.

"Bingle boo!" he said. "What—"

But he never got the chance to finish his sentence because, at that moment, the weirdest thing in the history of the world happened.

Mrs. Kormel must have leaned against the magic STOP sign button by accident. Because the magic STOP sign on the side of the bus swung out at the exact same time as Mr. Klutz arrived. The STOP sign smacked

Mr. Klutz on the side of his bald head! He fell down! It was a real Kodak moment.

Those STOP signs are dangerous!

We all rushed off the bus to see if Mr. Klutz was okay. He stood up slowly. He looked like he'd been in a fight, or he'd drunk too much beer.

"W-what happened?" he asked.

"The STOP sign hit you in the head," said Mrs. Kormel. "I'm so sorry."

"No, I mean why were you so late?" asked Mr. Klutz.

Everybody started telling Mr. Klutz what happened.

"We had a flat tire!"

"We got kidnapped and drove to the North Pole!"

"We went to the nude kid's house!"

"A.J. threw a doll out the window!"

"Ryan ate his seat cushion!"

"We got lost in the rainforest!"

"We pushed the bus out of a ditch!"

"We had a funeral for Striker Smith's head!"

"Well, I'm just glad you're all safe!" said Mr. Klutz.

"Did we miss the big spelling test?" asked Andrea.

"Oh, your teacher Miss Daisy was out sick today," said Mr. Klutz. "So your class had a substitute teacher named Ms. Todd. You'll have your spelling test tomorrow."

"Yippee!" yelled all the girls.

"Boo!" yelled all the boys.

While we were yelling, the school bell rang. The front door opened, and kids started pouring out.

"It's three o'clock!" said Mr. Klutz. "Everybody back on the bus. It's time to go home."

"Home?" said Andrea. "But we just *got* here!"

"Bix blattinger!" yelled Mrs. Kormel.

"Hey, wait a minute," I said to Mr. Klutz. "Where's the nude kid?"

"Nude kid?" said Mr. Klutz. "What are you talking about, A.J.?"

"You know," I said, "the kid we were going to pick up before we got lost."

"Ohhhhh!" said Mr. Klutz. "You mean the *new* kid. He's not nude. He's *new*. Here he comes now."

This kid came over to the bus. He looked pretty normal. He even had clothes on.

"What's your name?" Ryan asked him.

"Neil."

"Really?" Michael asked.

"Yeah, my name is Neil Crouch."

"Is that your *real* name?" I asked. "Neil Crouch?"

"Sure it is," he said. "Why?"

"Well," I explained, "if your name is Neil Crouch, that means you can kneel and crouch on the bus."

"Why would anybody want to kneel or crouch on a bus?" asked Neil Crouch.

"Because we're not allowed to!" we all yelled.

Sheesh! The nude kid has a lot to learn about being a kid. He's weird. Me and

Michael and Ryan decided to keep calling Neil Crouch "the nude kid" even if he did wear clothes.

We all got back in the bus, and Mrs. Kormel pulled out of the driveway. Maybe she'll get us back home before we die of starvation. Maybe we'll find out what "bix blattinger" means. Maybe I'll talk my parents into getting me another Striker Smith action figure. Maybe Neil Crouch will learn how to be a kid. Maybe I'll pass the big spelling test tomorrow.

But it won't be easy!